VILLAGE

Merry Christmas,
Kristina

(with love from

Elizabeth (et al.)

1988

MERRYDALE TREASURE HUNT

LINDA JENNINGS

ILLUSTRATED BY LAINI

· **Derrydale Books** ·
New York

L ong ago, when your great-grandparents were young, there were two small twins called Edward and Becky. They lived at the rectory in Merrydale Village.

One morning, the twins woke up with a lovely, excited, fluttery feeling inside them.

'Rise and shine, sleepy heads,' called their mother. She pulled back the curtains and the sun shone through the window. 'It's your birthday, and it's a lovely day.'

The twins immediately sprang out of bed, dressed, and rushed downstairs. But where were their presents?

'Don't look so sad,' said Mother, laughing.
'You are going to have a treasure hunt this year.'
She handed the twins a white card with some
writing on it.

'This is your first clue,' she said. 'You must look for four more clues somewhere in Merrydale Village. The last one will tell you where to find your birthday present.'

Edward and Becky ran out into the sunshine, clutching the white card their mother had given them. Edward asked his sister to read it.

'My shop is very near,
You can buy some chocolate here.'

'Mrs Greenacre sells chocolate,' cried Edward.

The twins raced as fast as they could across the
green to the sweetshop.

Mrs Greenacre, the shopkeeper, was behind the counter when the twins burst into the shop.

'Is there a white card here?' gasped Becky.

'With a clue on it?' said Edward.

Then Becky spotted the card underneath a large jar of bullseyes.

'Well done, my dears,' beamed Mrs Greenacre, giving them the card. 'And here's my little present for you, too.' She gave them two sticky, twisty sticks of barley-sugar.

Edward read the next clue with his mouth full of barley-sugar.

'*Clippety-clop goes a horse down the street,*
I make shoes to fit horses' feet.'

'The blacksmith,' they both shouted together.

They set off briskly down the lane, passing the gates of the Squire's house where two stone lions sat on the gateposts.

'They are guarding the house,' said Becky. She liked the lions.

The blacksmith was shoeing a horse as the twins poked their heads over the door.

'I can see the card,' said Edward at once, pointing to a saddle hanging on the wall. The card was pinned to the saddle and showed up against the dark leather.

'If it isn't the terrible twins,' cried the blacksmith, handing them the card. 'And here's a birthday present from me.' He gave them two beautiful shiny horseshoes. 'Horseshoes are lucky,' he said.

The next clue said:

If you write a letter to a far-away friend,
You bring it here for me to send.

'The Post Office,' guessed Becky.

Running back up the lane, the twins arrived at the Post Office, breathless. Inside, there was a small queue, and the children found it difficult to wait for their turn.

At last Miss Pennyquick was free, and at that very moment Edward saw a white card underneath the letter-weighing machine.

Miss Pennyquick handed it to him and said, 'I have a pile of cards and parcels for you. Shall I send them up to the rectory?'

'Yes please,' answered Edward.

Miss Pennyquick gave them each a brand-new spinning-top.

Becky read the next clue as Edward leant
against the village pump.

'*Carts and cows, tops and toys,*
I make these for girls and boys.'

'That's our friend, Tom,' exclaimed Edward.
'He makes marvellous wooden toys.

The two of them ran off through the churchyard to a row of cottages. The gardens were full of flowers and people were working in the morning sunshine.

A boy sat on the doorstep of the end cottage busily carving a piece of wood.

'You are clever, Tom,'said Becky.
She gasped with delight as he gave
them both a wooden cow he had
made for their toy farm. Then Becky saw the card.
'Can I take the clue out of your pocket, please,' she
asked politely. She read aloud:

'Go past the ducks, then look for me.
I'll be under the chestnut tree.'

'That's the last clue,' Tom said, but Edward and Becky did not hear him. They were already running down the lane to find the chestnut tree and their birthday present. They were tired now, but also very excited.

'It must mean Meadowsweet Farm,' said Becky. 'That has an enormous chestnut tree.'

They ran all the way down the track to the farmyard. As the children rushed past the duck pond the ducks swam away, quacking. A cow mooed at them over the hawthorn hedge.

'There's the chestnut tree,' they both cried.

They could hardly believe their eyes.
Underneath the chestnut tree stood the sweetest
little Shetland pony they had ever seen.

Then their mother and father came up the farm
track, pulling behind them yet another surprise.

'It's a trap!' cried the twins. 'Now we have our
very own pony and trap!'

When the pony had been harnessed to the trap, Edward and Becky climbed in and drove back up the track towards Merrydale Village.

'This is the best birthday present ever,' said Edward happily.

And Becky agreed.

First published in 1986 by Octopus Books Limited
This 1987 edition published by Derrydale Books
Distributed by Crown Publishers, Inc.,
225 Park Avenue South,
New York,
New York 10003

© Copyright 1986 Octopus Books Limited

ISBN 0-517-65133-5

Printed in the United Kingdom

The Rising Sun

MERRY